For my grandparents, Ruth and Eliot –D. B.
For Charlie & Amy –D. P.

STERLING CHILDREN'S BOOKS
New York

An Imprint of Sterling Publishing Co., Inc.
1166 Avenue of the Americas
New York, NY 10036

Text © 2016 by Donald Budge
Illustrations © 2016 by Daron Parton

ISBN 978-1-4549-1697-0

Distributed in Canada by Sterling Publishing Co., Inc.
℅ Canadian Manda Group, 664 Annette Street
Toronto, Ontario, Canada M6S 2C8
Distributed in the United Kingdom by GMC Distribution Services
Castle Place, 166 High Street, Lewes, East Sussex, England BN7 1XU

For information about custom editions, special sales, and premium and corporate purchases,
please contact Sterling Special Sales at 800-805-5489 or specialsales@sterlingpublishing.com.

Manufactured in China

Lot #:
4 6 8 10 9 7 5
12/18

www.sterlingpublishing.com

Designed by Philip Buchanan

Where Is My Butt?

by
DONALD BUDGE

illustrated by
DARON PARTON

STERLING CHILDREN'S BOOKS
New York

In a cold land far, far away, there lived a penguin named Morty. One day, he stood up and wondered, "Where is my butt?"

"I have never seen it. Or felt it."

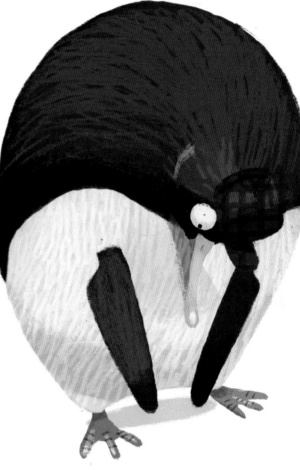

Morty tried to see and touch it.

But his flippers were too short to reach.

He couldn't remember sitting,
although he had thought about it.
"Do I have a butt?" Morty wondered.

He asked his best friend, Cornelius. "Do we have butts?
I have never seen or touched mine."

"What is a butt?" Cornelius asked. Cornelius was not very helpful.

He asked the other penguins,
"Where is my butt?"

Across the ice, Morty spotted an unfamiliar furry friend.
"Maybe the polar bear knows," Morty thought.
"Excuse me, Mr. Polar Bear," Morty asked,
approaching the polar bear. "I have a question."

"We can't be talking. You can't
see me," Mr. Polar Bear said.

"But you're right here!"
Morty exclaimed.

"No, I'm not," Mr. Polar Bear said.
"Polar bears only live in the North Pole,
and penguins only live in the South Pole."

"Where did he go?"

With the Polar Bear gone, Morty decided to ask the seal who lived by the ocean. "Perhaps the seal can help," Morty thought.

"Hello, Mr. Seal," Morty said. "Where is my butt? I do not know where it is."

Mr. Seal stared at Morty.

Morty stared back.

Mr. Seal lunged at Morty!
Morty screamed and dived into the water.

How rude! Maybe the other animals knew.

Under water, Morty decided to ask nearby friends. "Excuse me, sir," Morty asked. "Do you know where a butt might be?"

Jellyfish don't talk very much.

He swung through the jungle.

"Pardon me," Morty said to a native stranger.
"Could you help me solve a mystery?"

Morty then flew into space.
There he spotted some new friends.
Maybe they knew where a butt was

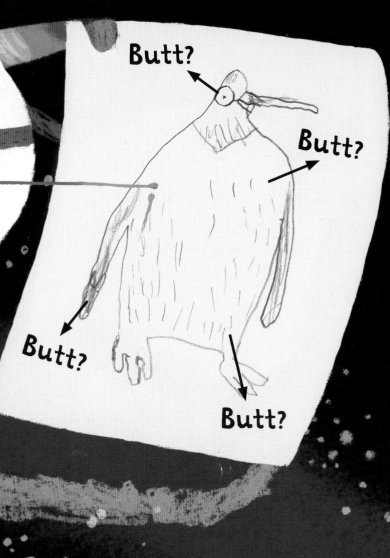

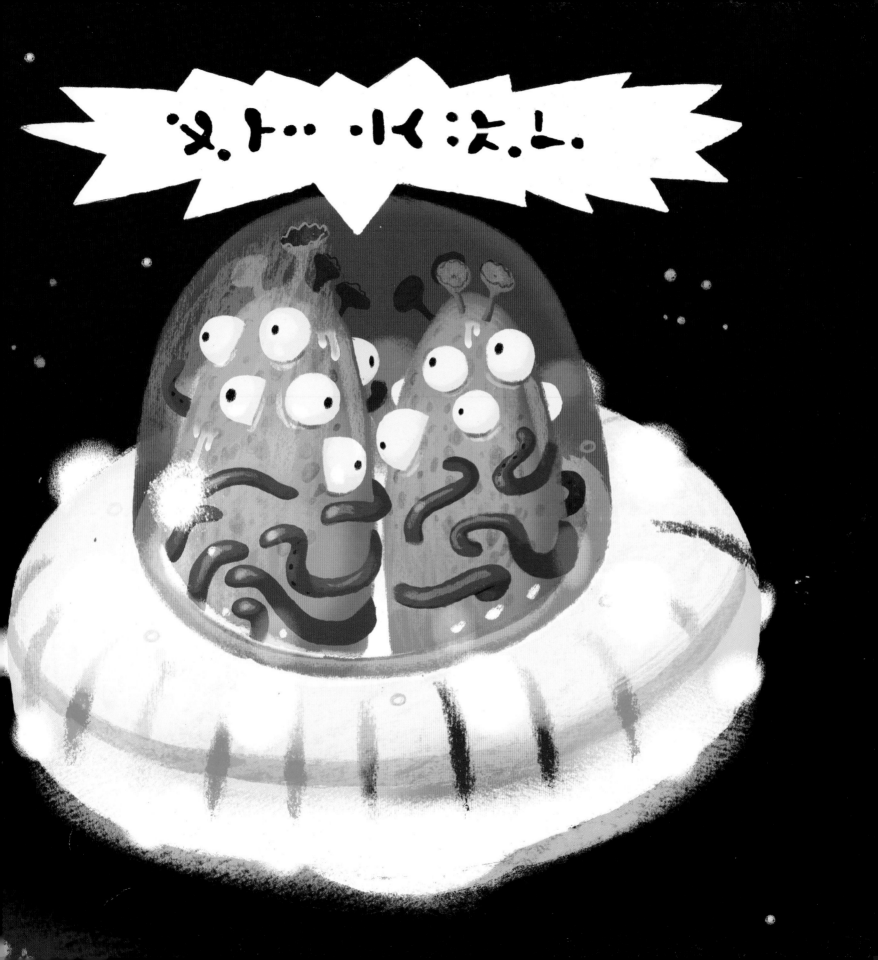

When that didn't work,
Morty traveled everywhere trying to find the solution.

But he still couldn't find his butt,
so he decided to do some experiments.

But even after all that,
Morty was still clueless.

"I still can't find my butt," Morty
thought sadly. "Maybe I don't have
one. I guess I'll go home."

Hungry from his travels, Morty prepared his usual fish dinner. As he ate, Morty thought, "I wish I could figure out where my butt is."

Suddenly, he felt a rumbling in his stomach.

He swung through the jungle.

"Pardon me," Morty said to a native stranger.
"Could you help me solve a mystery?"